For Benjamin    Para Benjamin
—Love, Tía Monica

Text copyright © 2016 by Monica Brown
Illustrations copyright © 2016 by Sara Palacios
Spanish translation copyright © 2016 by Lee & Low Books Inc.

Spanish translation by Adriana Domínguez
Book design by Carl Angel
Book production by The Kids at Our House
The text is set in Perpetua
The illustrations are rendered in mixed media, then
digitally enhanced

Manufactured in China by Imago, March 2016
Printed on paper from responsible sources
10 9 8 7 6 5 4 3 2 1
First Edition

# Marisol McDonald and the Monster

## Marisol McDonald y el monstruo

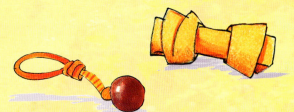

story / cuento **Monica Brown**

illustrations / ilustraciones **Sara Palacios**

Spanish translation / traducción al español **Adriana Domínguez**

Children's Book Press, *an imprint of* Lee & Low Books Inc.

New York

**M**y name is Marisol McDonald and I like words that begin with the letter **m**.

I like being **m**ismatched and **m**arvelous. And I love eating **m**angoes and *melocotones* and drinking **m**ilk with *m*iel!

**M**e llamo Marisol McDonald y me gustan las palabras que comienzan con la letra **m**.

Me gusta ser diferente y **m**aravillosa. ¡Me encanta comer **m**angos y **m**elocotones y tomar *milk* con **m**iel!

I especially like **M**onday **m**ornings, when I get ready for school. Over the weekends, I miss my favorite *m*aestra, **M**s. Apple, and our class **m**ouse, **M**illie the **M**ighty.

At school I love art and science and **m**ath. And English and Spanish too, because I get to use lots of my favorite **m** words: *m*agic, *m*ustard, *m*oon, *m*onkey, *m*ami, *m*aíz, *m*agnífico!

And of course I love to swing on the **m**onkey bars too.

Sobre todo, me encantan los lunes por la **m**añana, cuando me preparo
para ir a la escuela. Durante el fin de semana, extraño a mi **m**aestra
favorita, la Srta. Apple y a nuestra ratoncita **m**ascota, Súper **M**illie.

En la escuela, me encantan el arte, la ciencia y la **m**atemática. También
el inglés y el español, porque puedo usar muchas de mis palabras
favoritas con **m**: ¡*m*agic, *m*ustard, *m*oon, *m*onkey, **m**ami, **m**aíz, **m**agnífico!

Y por supuesto, también me encanta hacer **m**onerías en el pasamanos.

But there is one **m** word I do not like at all, and that word is . . . MONSTER!

I know monsters aren't real, but when I think of them, I see scary eyes and wild fur and pointy claws and sharp teeth.

Pero hay una palabra que empieza con **m** que no me gusta para nada, y es: ¡MONSTRUO!

Sé que los monstruos no existen, pero cuando pienso en ellos, me imagino ojos espantosos, cuerpos peludos, garras puntiagudas y dientes filosos.

mano

mo

One night when I'm just about to fall asleep, I hear a loud *BUMP*, and then another.

"Mami! Dad! There's a MONSTER under my bed! I hear it!" I yell, pulling the covers over my head.

Dad peeks below the bed. "No monster here," he says.

"Can Kitty sleep in my room, *¿por favor?*" I ask. "Please?" Kitty is the best dog ever. He could be my guard dog.

"Sorry, Marisol," Dad says. "Kitty's sleeping in his own bed downstairs."

Mami stays with me until I fall asleep, but it takes a long time.

Una noche, cuando estaba a punto de dormirme, sentí un fuerte ¡BUM! Y luego otro.

—¡Mami! ¡Dad! ¡Hay un monstruo debajo de mi cama! ¡Lo puedo oír! —grito, escondiéndome debajo de las cobijas.

Dad mira debajo de mi cama y dice:
—Aquí no veo un monstruo.

—¿Puede dormir Minino en mi cuarto, por favor? —les pido—. *Please?* Minino es el mejor perro del mundo. Él podría protegerme.

—Lo siento Marisol —dice Dad—. Minino debe dormir abajo, en su propia cama.

Mami se queda conmigo hasta que me duermo, pero demoro mucho en hacerlo.

The next night the same thing happens. I hear bumps,
I yell, and Dad checks under my bed. No monster.

Dad stays with me until I fall asleep.

It's the same the night after that and the night after that.
By Saturday we're all pretty tired. Except Kitty, who
wants to play ball.

"Do you think all monsters are scary?" I ask Kitty, but he
only barks.

A la noche siguiente sucede lo mismo. Oigo ruidos, grito y Dad mira debajo de mi cama. No ve ningún monstruo.

Dad se queda conmigo hasta que me duermo.

Esto sigue noche tras noche. Cuando llega el sábado, todos estamos bastante cansados. Menos Minino, que quiere jugar a la pelota.

—¿Piensas que todos los monstruos son espantosos? —le pregunto a Minino, pero él solo ladra.

In the afternoon I help Mami make empanadas, my most favorite dinner in the whole wide world. Mami lets me make them into different shapes.

"If monsters were real, would they have *mamis*?" I ask.

"Good question," Mami says. "What do you think, *amor*?"

Mami always likes to answer my questions with more questions.

Por la tarde, ayudo a mami a hacer empanadas, la cena que más me gusta en todo el mundo. Mami me deja darles diferentes formas.

—Si los monstruos existieran, ¿tendrían mamis? —le pregunto.

—Buena pregunta —contesta mami—. ¿Qué piensas tú, amor?

A mami le gusta contestar mis preguntas con más preguntas.

After dinner, my big brother, Juan, and I do the dishes.

"What do monsters look like?" I ask. "Do they all have scary eyes and wild fur and pointy claws and sharp teeth?"

"Marisol," Juan says. "You're too old to believe in monsters."

I frown. Nobody wants to talk to me about monsters. Not even my little brother, Gustavo.

I know monsters aren't real, but I can *imagine* them, and that makes them real enough to me.

Después de la cena, mi hermano mayor Juan y yo lavamos los platos.

—¿Cómo son los monstruos? —le pregunto—. ¿Tienen ojos espantosos, cuerpos peludos, garras puntiagudas y dientes filosos?

—Marisol —contesta Juan—, ya eres demasiado grande para creer en monstruos.

Me enojo porque nadie quiere hablar conmigo sobre los monstruos. Ni siquiera mi hermanito Gustavo.

Sé que los monstruos no existen, pero los puedo *imaginar* y eso hace que existan para mí.

Suddenly I have an idea. I can make my own monster, and I can imagine her any way I want! She will be *unique*, *different*, and *one of a kind*.

I take my markers, a few of Juan's old soccer socks, and some colorful yarn from Mami's knitting bag. Mami helps me sew up my monster, and I dress her in a purple polka-dot skirt and a green-striped shirt. I sew on three legs so she will be extra good at soccer. And I give her red hair, just like me, and blue fingernails!

De pronto, tengo una idea. ¡Puedo crear mi propia monstrua y la puedo imaginar como yo quiera! Va a ser original, diferente y única.

Tomo mis marcadores, unas medias viejas de fútbol de Juan y unas tiras de lana de colores de la bolsa de tejer de mami. Mami me ayuda a coser mi monstrua y yo le pongo una falda con lunares morados y una blusa rayada verde. Le pego tres piernas para que pueda jugar al fútbol súper bien. Luego le añado el cabello pelirrojo, como el mío, ¡y uñas azules!

I name my monster **M**elody, because that's a nice name and Melody is a nice monster. Who says monsters have to be scary or mean, anyway? Probably the same people who think purple polka dots and green stripes don't match.

Then I make a cardboard box into a little house for Melody. Gustavo helps me decorate it with hearts and peace signs. Melody's house fits right under my bed.

That night I fall asleep fast. I know there's a monster under my bed, but it's my very own monster.

Le pongo **M**elodía porque es un nombre bonito y Melodía es una monstrua buena. ¿Quién dice que los monstruos deben ser espantosos o malos? Probablemente las mismas personas que dicen que los lunares morados y las rayas verdes no combinan.

Luego, convierto una caja de cartón en una casita para Melodía. Gustavo me ayuda a decorarla con corazones y signos de la paz. La casa de Melodía cabe justo debajo de mi cama.

Esa noche, me duermo rápido. Sé que hay un monstruo debajo de mi cama, pero es mi propio monstruo.

But then, in the middle of the night, I hear a really loud *BUMP*, and all of a sudden I'm wide-awake.

I open my mouth to yell for Mami and Dad, but I don't need to. They are already in my room, and my brothers are right behind them.

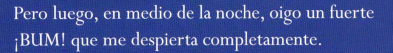

Pero luego, en medio de la noche, oigo un fuerte ¡BUM! que me despierta completamente.

Abro la boca para llamar a mami y a Dad pero no es necesario. Ellos ya están en mi cuarto, junto con mis hermanos.

PERÚ

'We hear it too," Dad says, just as there's another
*BUMP! BUMP!*

And then . . . *BUMPITY BUMP!*

'I think it's coming from downstairs," I say.

We tiptoe down the stairs. I bring Melody with me
in case she's scared to be by herself.

—Nosotros también lo oímos —dice Dad, justo en el momento en que se oye otro ¡BUM! ¡BUM!

Y luego: ¡BÚMPITI BUM!

—¡Creo que viene de abajo! —digo yo.

Bajamos juntos de puntitas. Traigo a Melodía conmigo, en caso de que tenga miedo de quedarse sola.

BUMP!

BUMP!

BUMPITY
BUMP!

¡BUM!

¡BUM!

¡BÚMPITI
BUM!

As we get closer to the kitchen, the *BUMP*s get louder.

Dad turns on the light.

Kitty is not asleep in his bed. Kitty is playing with his ball, pushing it against the wall with his nose.

A medida que nos acercamos a la cocina, los ¡BUM! se oyen cada vez más fuertes.

Dad enciende la luz.

Minino no está durmiendo en su cama. Está jugando con su pelota, tirándola hacia la pared con la nariz.

It turns out the monster making noise under my bed does have eyes and fur and teeth, but he isn't scary at all! I give Kitty a great big hug. Then I look up at my parents.

"Mami, Dad," I say. "I think this monster needs company."

Resulta que el monstruo que oía debajo de mi cama sí
tiene ojos, piel y dientes, ¡pero no es nada espantoso!
Le doy un gran abrazo a Minino. Luego miro a mis papás.

—Mami, Dad —les digo—. Creo que este monstruo
necesita compañía.

## Author's Note

My bold, magical Marisol McDonald is a character born of two cultures who isn't afraid to be herself. Whether it's through her colorful artwork, her unconventional sense of fashion (Who wants to match? Not Marisol!), or her unique way of solving problems, Marisol has an imagination that is big and great and wild. This is a wonderful thing—most of the time. The mind is powerful at any age, and even older children can still be afraid of the dark or what it represents. When Marisol starts hearing loud bumps in the middle of the night, she imagines a monster, which is her way of naming her fear. With the support of her loving family, Marisol learns to face this fear and transform it in true, one-of-a-kind Marisol McDonald fashion. This book is for anyone—babies, kids, adults (including you and me!)—who has ever been afraid of anything.

## Nota de la autora

Mi audaz y mágica Marisol McDonald es un personaje que nació de dos culturas y que no tiene miedo a ser ella misma. Ya sea por medio de sus coloridos dibujos, su original sentido de la moda (¿Quién desea ir combinada? ¡Marisol seguro que no!), o su modo único de resolver problemas, la imaginación de Marisol es amplia y profunda. Esto es algo bueno, la mayor parte del tiempo. La mente es algo muy poderoso a cualquier edad, y aún niños un poco mayores son capaces de tenerle miedo a la oscuridad, o a lo que representa para ellos. Cuando Marisol comienza a oír ruidos fuertes en medio de la noche, se imagina un monstruo, lo cual es su forma de darle un nombre a su miedo. Con el apoyo de su cariñosa familia, Marisol aprende a confrontar este miedo y a transformarlo de una manera en que solo Marisol McDonald puede hacerlo. Este libro es para bebés, niños y adultos (¡hasta para ti y para mí!), es decir, para todos aquellos que en algún momento han sentido miedo por algo.

## Glossary

**Abuelita** (ah-bweh-LEE-tah): Grandma

**amor** (ah-MOR): love

**empanada** (em-pah-NAH-dah): turnover with a sweet
   or savory filling

**maestra** (mah-ES-trah): teacher

**magnífico** (mag-NEE-fee-koh): magnificent, wonderful

**maíz** (mah-EES): corn

**Mami** (MAH-mee): Mom

**mano** (MAH-noh): hand

**melocotón** (me-loh-coh-TOHN): peach

**mi casa** (me KAH-sah): my house

**miel** (mee-ehl): honey

**mono** (MOH-noh): monkey

**Perú** (pe-ROOH): Peru; country in South America

**por favor** (pohr fah-VOHR): please

## Glosario

**Dad** (dad): Papá

**Kitty** (QUI-ti): Minino

**magic** (MÁ-yik): mágico

**milk** (milk): leche

**monkey** (MON-qui): mono

**moon** (mun): luna

**mouse** (maus): ratón

**mustard** (MÓS-tard): mostaza

**please** (plis): por favor

**stickers** (STI-quers): calcomanías

**Monica Brown** is the author of many award-winning books for young readers, including the Marisol McDonald series, *Maya's Blanket / La manta de Maya*, and the Lola Levine series. The character of Marisol is inspired by Brown's own mixed racial and religious heritage, and by her desire to bring diverse stories to children. Brown is also a professor of English at Northern Arizona University, where she teaches US Latino/Latina and African American literature. She and her family live in Flagstaff, Arizona. Visit her online at monicabrown.net.

**Monica Brown** es la escritora de varios libros premiados para jóvenes, incluyendo la serie de Marisol McDonald, *Maya's Blanket / La manta de Maya* y la serie de Lola Levine. El personaje de Marisol fue inspirado por la herencia étnica y religiosa de la propia Brown, y su deseo de brindar historias diversas a los niños. Brown es profesora de ingles en la Universidad del Norte de Arizona, donde enseña literatura estadounidense latina y afroamericana. Brown vive con su familia en Flagstaff, Arizona. Visítala en su página Web: monicabrown.net.

**Sara Palacios** is the illustrator of the Marisol McDonald picture books. She created the beloved visual image of Marisol for the first book in the series, *Marisol McDonald Doesn't Match / Marisol McDonald no combina*, for which she won a Pura Belpré Illustrator Award Honor. Marisol, with her unique personality, is one of the most interesting characters with which she has worked, Palacios says. Palacios divides her time between Mexico City and San Francisco, California. Her website is sarapalaciosillustrations.com.

**Sara Palacios** es la ilustradora de la serie de Marisol McDonald. Elle creó la querida imagen visual de Marisol en el primer libro, llamado *Marisol McDonald Doesn't Match / Marisol McDonald no combina*, por el cual recibió el premio de honor Pura Belpré para ilustradores. Palacios dice que Marisol, con su personalidad única, es uno de los personajes más interesantes que ha ilustrado. Palacios divide su tiempo entre Ciudad de México y San Francisco, California. Su página Web es: sarapalaciosillustrations.com.

Library of Congress Cataloging-in-Publication Data
Names: Brown, Monica, 1969- | Palacios, Sara, illustrator. |
   Domínguez, Adriana, translator.
Title: Marisol McDonald and the monster / story, Monica
   Brown ; illustrations, Sara Palacios ; Spanish translation,
   Adriana Domínguez = Marisol McDonald y el monstruo /
   cuento, Monica Brown ; ilustraciones, Sara Palacios ;
   traducción al español, Adriana Domínguez.
Other titles: Marisol McDonald y el monstruo
Description: First edition. | New York : Children's Book Press,
   an imprint of Lee & Low Books Inc., [2016] | Summary: "A
spunky, bilingual, multiracial girl finds her own way to conquer
her fear of the nighttime monster that mysteriously appears
in her home. Includes author's note and glossary"— Provided
by publisher.
Identifiers: LCCN 2015024712 | ISBN 9780892393268
(hardcover : alk. paper)
Subjects: | CYAC: Monsters—Fiction. | Fear of the dark—
   Fiction. | Racially mixed people—Fiction. | Hispanic
   Americans—Fiction. | Spanish language materials—Bilingual.
Classification: LCC PZ73 .B685635 2016 | DDC [E]—dc23
LC record available at http://lccn.loc.gov/2015024712

AWP